*The* *Classical* *Spirit*

**Book 1**

Selected, edited and annotated by *Nancy Bachus*

**1750–1820**

**24 Early Intermediate to Intermediate Piano Solos**
**Reflecting Classical Society, Style and Musical Trends**

Alfred

Cover art: *George, 3rd Earl Cowper, with the Family of Charles Gore*
ca. 1775 by Johann Zoffany (1733–1810), Oil on canvas
Yale Center for British Art, Paul Mellon Collection, USA
Photo Credit/Bridgeman Art Library

# $\mathcal{C}$ontents

# Foreword

To understand and interpret musical style, one must recapture the spirit of the environment in which composers lived, created and performed, and be aware of influential events of the time. Johann Sebastian Bach's death in 1750 marks the end of the Baroque period, an era of distinctive musical style. While Bach was alive, his sons and other musicians of the time had already begun to write a new style of keyboard music. This new, simpler style was predominantly a melody-and-accompaniment texture; its primary purpose was to please or entertain.

During the late 18th century, secular music surpassed sacred in importance. More instrumental than vocal music was written; the piano edged out the harpsichord as the favorite keyboard instrument. Political revolution and social changes brought a decreased reliance on patrons. A new music industry was developing in which musicians began to earn their living by publishing their compositions, performing and teaching. The public now wanted to hear music as a form of entertainment and acquire skills for personal music making. Early 18th-century trends culminated in the works of three great Classical composers who lived and worked around Vienna: Franz Joseph Haydn, Wolfgang Amadeus Mozart and Ludwig van Beethoven.

Many instruction books appeared in the 18th century that explained the various aspects of musical performance and composition. Recent study of these has given greater insight into the way music was performed at the time.

---

**General Principles for Interpreting Articulation markings in Classical Style**

Classical touch:

- usually **nonlegato** unless marked with a slur
- slur marks indicate groupings within the larger phrase

The beginning of each Classical slur group should have a gentle emphasis, with a lift only at the end of the larger musical unit (phrase or musical sentence).

Correct 18th-century interpretation:

Incorrect 18th-century interpretation:

---

The German theorist and composer, **Daniel Gottlob Türk** (1750–1813), states in his 1789 *Clavierschule* (*The School of Keyboard Playing*) that all tones, even rapid passages, must be **cleanly separated**.[1] Similarities between music and speech are drawn, and he vividly illustrates how meaning is changed through groupings and emphasis with the sentence, *"He lost his life, not only his fortune,"* and *"He lost his life not, only his fortune."*[2] By changing a comma, a different idea is conveyed. The way music is articulated contributes greatly to its expression.

---

[1] Daniel Gottlob Türk, *Clavierschule (The School of Keyboard Playing)*, trans., intro. and notes by Raymond H. Haggh (Lincoln: University of Nebraska Press, 1982), 324.
[2] Ibid., 329.

# Classic, Classical and Classicism

**Classic, classical and classicism,** in the strictest sense, refer to the language, art and culture of the **ancient Greeks and Romans.** More broadly, these terms refer to any style or creative work with characteristics derived from them. The ancient Greeks tried to understand human beings' roles in the world, their actions and values. Their conclusions became the basis for thinking about many issues in Western civilization.

In Greece, a man's knowledge of music often determined his rank in society and nobility. Slaves were prohibited from its practice. **Music was a part of the curriculum** intended to give young men moral strength and orderly minds. Winners of musical competitions were national heroes. Greek attitudes toward music became part of the foundation for Western music, although almost none of their actual music has survived.

*A musician from ancient (classical) Greece playing on a **lyre**. In mythology Hermes, a messenger of the gods, made the first lyre from an empty tortoise shell.*

- Originally, the term *classicus* referred to classes in Roman society, especially to the highest class of people, things and achievements.

- Today, a **classic** is someone (or something) recognized as setting a **standard of excellence,** of high class or quality, and of enduring value. It is used to refer to art, music, literary works, fashion and sports and is associated with things that are more traditional than experimental in style.

- In a generic sense, **"classical"** music refers to all **art music** (Western music from the 15th through the 20th centuries), in contrast to **"popular" music.**

*Musicians performing "classical" music*

*"Music has the power of producing a certain effect on the moral character of the soul, and if it has the power to do this, it is clear that the young must be directed to music and must be educated in it."*

Aristotle (384–322 BC), Greek philosopher[3]

# Classical Style Period (1750–1820)

The **Classical period** refers to music of the late 18th and early 19th centuries, and in the strictest sense, to the mature works of **Franz Joseph Haydn** (1732–1809), **Wolfgang Amadeus Mozart** (1756–1791), and the early works of **Ludwig van Beethoven** (1770–1827). Since they worked primarily in Vienna, Austria, Haydn, Mozart and Beethoven are known as the **Viennese Masters**. Some music historians include music by all composers from the mid-1700s to the early 1800s as part of the Classical period.

*Musicians from the Classical period performing music*

*"Dare to know! Have courage to use your understanding! That is the motto of enlightenment."*

Immanuel Kant (1724–1804), German philosopher[4]

## The Enlightenment

The Enlightenment was an **intellectual movement**, begun in France in the early 1700s. Its philosophy was that the power of reason should be applied to all aspects of human life—politics, government, religion, education, the arts.

- The philosophers of this movement wanted information gathered, classified, collated and available to all. **Denis Diderot** (1713–1784) published an *Encyclopédie* between 1751 and 1772 for the purpose of *"assemble[ing] the knowledge...of the earth."*[5] They believed in humanity's natural goodness, and that conditions in society could be improved through knowledge.

- The philosophers believed the power of a monarch or government should depend upon the will of the people, with men and women free to achieve their full potential. These ideals planted the seeds for political revolution.

[3]Ian Crofton & Donald Fraser, *A Dictionary of Musical Quotations* (New York: Schirmer Books, 1985), 55.
[4]William Fleming, *Art and Ideas* (Orlando, FL: Holt, Rinehart and Winston, 1991), 421.
[5]Denis Diderot, *Encylopédie* (New York: Dover Publications, Inc., 1993, reprint), x.

## Neo-Classicism in Art and Architecture

Archaeological excavations from Rome in the 1740s renewed interest in the ancient world. Eighteenth-century intellectuals idealized **Greek and Roman civilizations**.

- Ancient art (and the political ideals of republican Rome) became a model for 18th-century artists and intellectuals. Its dignity and "noble simplicity" made Rococo art appear frivolous and overdone.

- A **Neo-classic[6] art** emerged as buildings were designed with straight lines and geometric shapes supported by columns according to **Greek and Roman proportions**. Classical columns are common in public buildings in the Western world today.

*This engraving is of the ruins of the Roman temple of Neptune. Sketched at the site by Jacques Soufflot in 1750, it was influential in the development of Neo-classic architecture throughout Europe and the United States.*

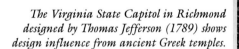

*The Virginia State Capitol in Richmond designed by Thomas Jefferson (1789) shows design influence from ancient Greek temples.*

The French artist, **Jacques-Louis David** (1748–1825), painted scenes from Roman history and reflected classical values in the symmetrical arrangement of figures around a focal point. On the eve of the French Revolution, there was also hidden political commentary in his paintings about current conditions in French society.

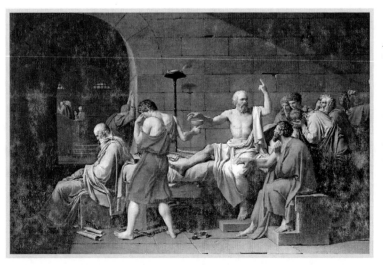

*Jacques-Louis David's* The Death of Socrates *(1787), points up Socrates's willingness to die for his beliefs; therefore encouraging lower-class French people to rise up against the aristocracy and, like Socrates, to make personal sacrifice, even die, for their ideals and for the greater good.*

---

[6] The prefix "neo" was used to describe the visual arts of this period to set them apart from antiquity. It is not necessary in the field of music since none exists from the earlier time period.

## Scientific Advancement

Life was changing for individuals during the 18th century with the basics established for scientific study in medicine and other fields. Better roads, improved stagecoaches and other developments were impacting daily routines.

—**Benjamin Franklin** (1706–1790) experimented with electricity (around 1750).
—**James Watt** (1736–1819) developed a high-powered steam engine (1769).
—**James Hargreaves** (1710–1778) patented his spinning jenny (1770).
—**Joseph Priestley** (1733–1804) discovered oxygen (1774).
—**Eli Whitney** (1765–1825) invented the cotton gin (1793).
—**Edward Jenner** (1749–1823) perfected smallpox vaccinations (1796).

## The Early Industrial Revolution and Its Affect on Musical Life

Scientific discoveries affected people's lives as machines and factories replaced hand tools and created new products.

- With improvements in sanitation, medicine and nutrition, the plagues and famines of the past had decreased and **population was increasing in Europe**.

- More food was produced by fewer farmers due to new methods and tools in agriculture. The beginnings of the Industrial Revolution created new service and manufacturing jobs, and **urban areas were increasing in size.**

- Improved manufacturing techniques made **musical instruments and music available and affordable** to an increasingly wealthy and powerful middle class. A public willing to pay for music lessons and concerts was developing.

*An 18th-century French instrument-maker's workshop (from Diderot's* Encyclopédie).

## Trends in the Classical Period

Musical life throughout Europe at this time **reflected international culture**. Musicians traveled and **Italian** opera composers and singers, **French** dancers and dancing masters, and **German** conductors and instrumentalists were dominant in all countries.

Musicians valued qualities found in ancient art and the Enlightenment: symmetry and balance of formal design, simplicity or naturalness, and expressivity limited by the bounds of good taste.

**Instrumental music surpassed vocal music** in quantity and strived to be **noble** as well as **entertaining. Orchestras expanded** in size and eliminated the harpsichord. The **improved pianoforte** became the fashionable keyboard instrument of the day.

# Classical Ornamentation

Classical musicians used **fewer, and less frequent ornaments** than in the recent past, and ornaments were gradually absorbed into the written score. Treatises of the time gave instruction on ornaments, but they vary on exact notation and execution. The following are generally accepted realizations of common Classical ornaments.

*Any of these realizations for ornaments could vary within a specific musical context. Speed of execution depends upon the rhythm, tempo and character of the music.*

| Common Classical Ornaments (German Symbols) | | | | | | |
|---|---|---|---|---|---|---|
| | Symbol | Beginning Note | Number of Notes | Direction | Rhythmic Beginning | Execution |
| **Mordent** | | written note | 3 | down | on the beat | |
| **Trill** | or *tr* | note above | 4 or more depending on the length of the ornamented note | down | on the beat | |
| **Schneller**[7] | | written note | 3 | up | on the beat | |
| **Turn** | | note above | 4 | down, then *turn* back up | where placed | |
| **Trilled turn** | | note above, but it's tied | 6 | down, then *turn* back up | on the beat | |

**Long Appoggiatura:** (leaning note) is played on the beat, thus delaying the principal note by half its length. If the principal note is a dotted note, the appoggiatura takes two thirds of its length.

With ordinary and dotted notes:

With a chord:

**Short Appoggiatura:** occurs most commonly before fast moving notes. It can be executed as a "crush," played on the beat, almost simultaneously with the principal note.

---

[7] The *Schneller* ("snap" or inverted mordent) has the same symbol as the trill. However, this ornament **begins on the main note.** It was used on fast moving notes when there was no time for a complete trill and/or to avoid striking consecutive notes in a descending line. Theorists of the time cautioned that it should not be overused.

# The Classical Minuet in Various Forms

*"Z" pattern of the minuet, showing pattern for dancers with verbal instructions for steps.[9]*

The most popular social dance in 18th-century Europe was the **minuet**. Many **keyboard minuets** were used for actual dancing while others were **stylized**; they had characteristics of the dance, but were not intended for dancing.

Books of **choreographic notation** were published in the early 18th century describing the court dances. In the minuet, a couple moved through an elaborate floor pattern along an imaginary letter Z.[8] When they passed in the middle, they presented right hands, turned and moved to opposite corners. Next, they presented left hands, and concluded with both hands.

*Presentation of the right hand in a minuet. Engraving from Kellom Tomlinson's* The Art of Dancing *(18th century)*

It could take months to make these patterns appear effortless. Those who could not perform in a graceful, dignified way were considered social failures. Originally danced by only one couple, at a later time, couples danced it simultaneously, circling each other holding right hands, then left, and finally the man led with both hands.

Most minuets were 16–32 measures in length. However, according to descriptions of the time, it took 100 measures to complete the dance. Accompanying **musicians repeated sections, improvised variations,** or **performed several minuets in succession**.

## Professional Women Musicians in the 18th Century

By the late 18th century, professional female musicians were **singing** in operas and court ballets, **appearing as instrumentalists** and **teaching music** to the nobility. Their most popular instruments were piano, violin, harp and guitar. A few women composed, and others were involved in music publishing and piano manufacturing.

---

[8]The "Z" was adapted by dancing masters from its original "S" (the sign for the Sun King, Louis XIV).
[9]Pierre Rameau, 1725.

**Elisabetta de Gambarini** was known in London primarily as a professional singer who performed in many of George Frideric Handel's (1685–1759) oratorios. She was also an organist, orchestral conductor and composer. This minuet is from her sixth *Sonata for Harpsichord.*

**Minuet form: binary or two-part**

Sections: ‖: A :‖: B :‖
       I  V  I  I

(In binary form, the first section cadences on a **V** chord.)

# Minuet in F Major

**Allegretto**

Elisabetta de Gambarini
(1731–1765)

SECTION A

Ⓐ Throughout this book, the editor suggests that all notes not marked with a slur be played nonlegato, with a slight separation. See the Foreword (page 3) for further details on 18th-century articulation.

**Johann Christoph Friedrich Bach**, the oldest son of Johann Sebastian Bach (1685–1750) and Anna Magdalena Bach (1701–1760), spent most of his life as a court musician in Bückenburg, Germany.

# Two Minuets

Johann Christoph Friedrich Bach
(1732–1795)

**Jan Ladislav Dussek**, born in Prague, was one of the first touring piano virtuosos appearing in St. Petersburg, Paris, London and many German cities. He studied with Carl Philipp Emanuel Bach (1714–1788), knew Muzio Clementi (1752–1832) and Franz Joseph Haydn, and was one of the first to produce a "singing tone" on the piano. His works were popular in his lifetime.

# Minuet with Variation

Jan Ladislav Dussek
(1760–1812)

## The Enlightenment in the United States of America

The American **Declaration of Independence** (1776) was an example of reasoned, classical thought. Instead of emotionally shouting, "Kill the King," the political leaders were logical, restrained and sensible as they wrote a legal brief listing the colonists' grievances. *When in the course of human events, it becomes necessary for one people to dissolve the political bands which have connected them with another...*

**Thomas Jefferson** (1743–1826) is a representation of the ideal, cultured **man of the Enlightenment** who did many things well. He was an excellent violinist, singer and dancer. Fluent in six languages, he translated several books, including the Bible, from the original languages. An accomplished architect and inventor, he applied science to farming and was knowledgeable about meteorology. His personal library became the nucleus for the Library of Congress.

While serving as Ambassador to France, Jefferson invited **Jean-Antoine Houdon** (1741–1828), a great **sculptor** of the time, to the United States. Houdon, who was known for his accurate portrayals, sculpted George Washington at Mt. Vernon.

*Houdon's images of Franklin, Jefferson and Washington
are found on the fifty-cent piece, nickel and quarter.*

## The Minuet in the United States of America

In the colonies, manners and customs, including music, were modeled after English society.

- A Governor's Ball was held on the King's birthday. Guests were often entertained with elaborate feasting and dancing, especially on Southern plantations. Daughters, servants and slaves provided the music.

- By 1700, music instructors and dancing masters, usually with a European background, were common.

- By 1750, concerts, operas, and musical evenings in homes or assembly halls were frequent in larger American cities. Immediately following many concerts, the instrumentalists would provide music for a formal ball, traditionally opened with a minuet.

- **George Washington** (1732–1799) enjoyed music, the theater, and especially dancing.

---

[10]Joseph Machlis & Kristine Forney, *The Enjoyment of Music* (New York: W. W. Norton & Co., 1995), 227.

Photo: The Library of Virginia

*George Washington (1788) by Jean-Antoine
Houdon. Richmond, Virginia, Capitol Building*

## Minuet and Trio

The most common form of the minuet in the Classical period was the **minuet and trio.**
The minuet and trio was the form frequently used for the **third movement of multi-
movement classical forms** (like sonata, symphony or string quartet). In performance
both sections of the minuet are repeated, followed by both sections of the trio. After the
trio, the minuet is traditionally played again without repeating the sections.

- Minuet and trio **similarities:** usually in binary form and about the same length.

- Minuet and trio **differences:** keys, theme, character and texture of the music.

(This is the form for the *Minuet Danced before Mrs. Washington* on the following page.)

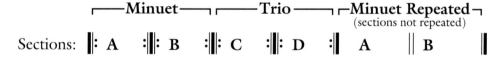

┌──Minuet──┐ ┌──Trio──┐ ┌Minuet Repeated┐
(sections not repeated)

Sections: ‖: A :‖: B :‖: C :‖: D :‖ A ‖ B ‖

La Dance

*Two engravings by Daniel Chodowiecki*

*The engraving on the right illustrates
the graceful dignity expected of 18th-century men and
women in contrast to the affected
and inappropriate gestures and stance
of the couple on the left.*

The French musician and dancing master, **Pierre Landrin Duport**, performed and taught in Philadelphia. This minuet is from a collection of dance tunes in the Library of Congress. It was performed *"by two young ladies in the presence of Mrs. Washington in 1792."*[11]

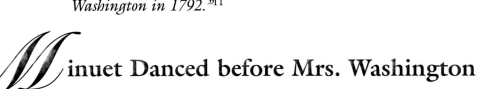

*An engraving of Martha Washington*

# Minuet Danced before Mrs. Washington

Pierre Landrin Duport
(1762–1841)

[11] Carl Engel, introduction to *Music from the Days of George Washington* (Washington, DC: George Washington Bicentennial Commission, 1931), viii.

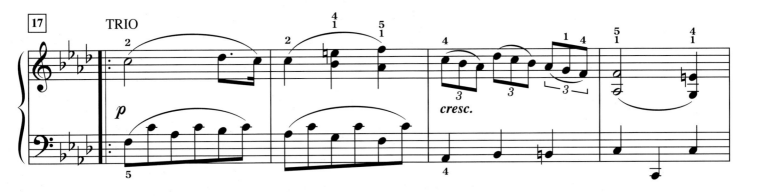

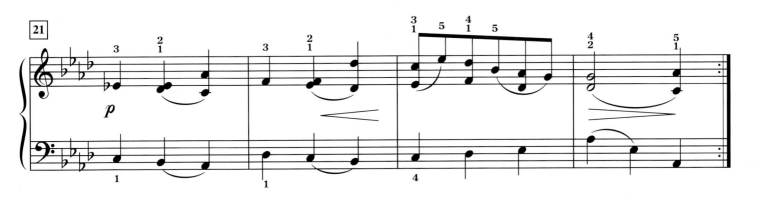

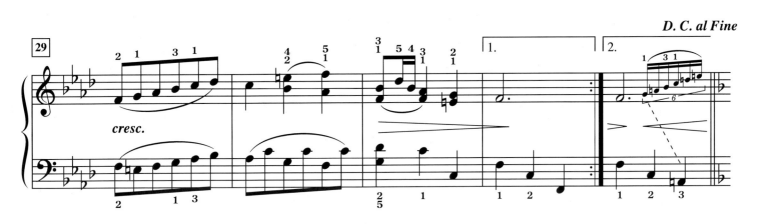

## Scherzo and Trio

By the mid-18th century, composers sometimes **replaced the minuet and trio with a scherzo and trio.** Ludwig van Beethoven used the title "scherzo" instead of "minuet" in most of his works. The form remained essentially the same, but scherzos were **faster** than minuets and, since scherzo literally means **joke**, the character of the music was more **humorous** and, at times, boisterous.

**Carl Maria von Weber** was a composer, conductor, music critic and one of the first to use the piano in a dramatic way in his compositions and as a virtuoso performer. Greatly influenced by Beethoven, Weber was a leader in the transition from Classical- to Romantic-style piano music.

# Scherzo

A. 10

Carl Maria von Weber
(1786–1826)

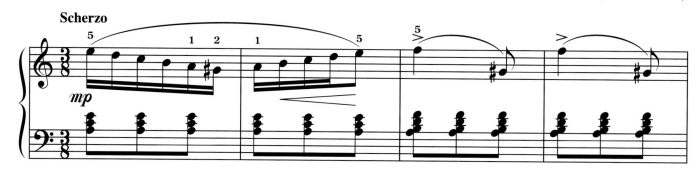

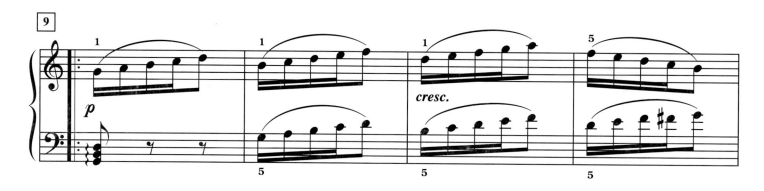

# Court of King Frederick the Great

**Frederick II, King of Prussia** (1712–1786), laid the foundation for modern Germany by expanding the power, territory and influence of Prussia during his 46-year reign. He did this through his military brilliance and his intellectual and artistic abilities and interests.

- Almost immediately after becoming King, he went to war, gained control over Silesia, and in later years won other territories as well.

- Frederick saw himself as the Greek philosopher, Plato's (ca. 428–347 B.C.) **enlightened philosopher-king,** allowing freedom of speech and religion, and establishing cultural institutions such as a science academy and the Berlin Opera.

- His Court in Berlin was French in language, manners, furnishings and architecture, yet he gathered the finest thinkers, artists, dancers and musicians from all of Europe. He practiced the flute four times a day and considered musical activities an escape from state duties. Arising at 4 a.m., most days ended with a late dinner and an evening concert where he performed some of the 300 flute concertos he knew.

**Carl Philipp Emanuel Bach** (1714–1788), Johann Sebastian's second and most famous son, was the principal keyboard player at the Court of Frederick the Great for nearly 30 years. C.P.E. Bach made a distinction between his father's **"learned,"** more contrapuntal style of composition, and the newer *style galant* favored by composers of his generation. *Galant* music, usually performed in small, intimate settings, had a freer texture and was frequently written for female amateurs.

*Flute Concerto at Sans Souci by Adolf von Menzel.*
*King Frederick the Great playing the flute*
*accompanied by C.P.E. Bach at the keyboard.*

# Characteristics of *Style Galant* or Classical Style Music

One aspect of the newer *style galant,* also characteristic of Classical-style music, is a **balanced phrase structure** with a melody divided into **short two- to four-measure segments** set off by cadences. The following *Allegro in G Major* has many two-measure melodic segments that begin with a pick-up note.

---

[12] Giles Macdonogh, *Frederick the Great* (New York: St. Martin's Press, 2000), jacket.

# 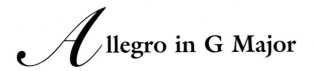llegro in G Major

Carl Philipp Emanuel Bach
(1714–1788)

While employed at the Court in Berlin, **C.P.E. Bach** published many keyboard works for the general public. Among them were *"musical portraits of several young ladies known to him in the form of short keyboard pieces...people...have assured me that their temperament has been expressed."*[13] A **harmonized melody** predominates and is another characteristic of *style galant* and Classical-style music.

# La Caroline

Carl Philipp Emanuel Bach
(1714–1788)

ⓐ The editor suggests playing a **Schneller** in this piece.

[13] Hans-Günter Ottenberg, *Carl Philipp Emanuel Bach*, quoting from the introduction to the first issue dated Nov. 22, 1760 (New York: Oxford University Press, 1991), 102.

**Georg Anton Benda** played violin in Frederick the Great's orchestra. He traveled to Italy, France and Austria and composed operas and church music as well as many songs and keyboard pieces. This **one-movement sonatina** (small sonata) is in binary form, similar to the sonatas of Domenico Scarlatti (1685–1757). One **rhythmic motive** dominates.

# Sonatina in D Major

Georg Anton Benda
(1722–1795)

> *"More can be lost by poor fingering than can be replaced by all conceivable artistry and good taste."*
>
> C.P.E. Bach[14]

**C.P.E. Bach** published keyboard music in a wide variety of styles. This *Presto in C Minor* is from a 1768 collection called *Short and Easy Piano Pieces with Varied Repetitions*. In this piece, the **A¹** section (measures 17–32) is a **varied repetition** of the **A** section (measures 1–16). Likewise, **B¹** (measures 57–72) is a varied repetition of **B** (measures 33–56).

# Presto in C Minor

Carl Philipp Emanuel Bach
(1714–1788)
Wq. 114/3

[14]Kathleen Kimball, ed., *The Music Lover's Quotation Book* (Toronto: Sound and Vision, 1990), 86.

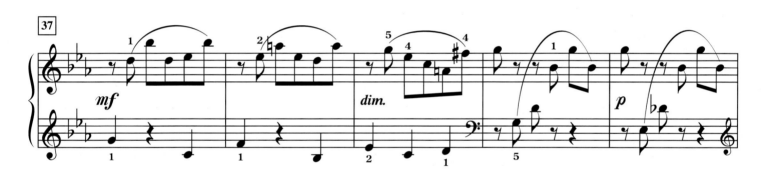

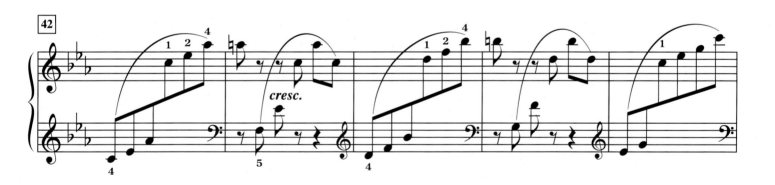

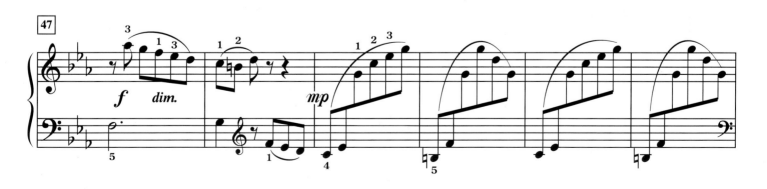

*"[A clavichord]...is tender and responsive to your soul's every inspiration,...here you will find your heart's soundboard...in the contact with those wonderful strings and caressing keys."*

Christian Schubart (1739–1791), German composer and poet[15]

## *Empfindsamkeit* (Sensitive/Sentimental Style)

In North Germany in the mid-1700s, there was a movement to create sensitive, emotional expression or "true and natural" feelings in music. It was a reaction to more rational *"melodies that say nothing and merely tickle the ear,"*[16] and of *"music that falls on the ear and fills it up, but leaves the heart empty."*[17]

- The leading exponent of this style in keyboard music was C.P.E. Bach who believed the purpose of music was to *"move the heart..."*[18] He wanted to move quickly from one emotion to another without speech. To accomplish this, he used dissonance, sudden changes in keys, dynamics and harmonies; contrasting themes, and sections in free rhythm, which, in his lifetime, many found to be bizarre. His music has an improvisatory quality with sections of instrumental recitatives and cadenza-like passages. This is evident in his **fantasias**.

*A large clavichord, popular in 18th-century Germany*

**To My Clavier**
*Thou faithful stringed array,*
*Echo my sighing soul!...*
*Fond strings, obey my hand,*
*Help me my pain withstand*—[19]

*Eighteenth-century German songbooks had many poems similar to this in various musical settings.*

- C.P.E. Bach's favorite keyboard instrument for personal use was the **clavichord**, and he had a large one built to his specifications.

- The clavichord's simple construction (a metal tangent on the end of the key) made it inexpensive. It was especially popular with German families.

- The tone was small (about *ppp* to *p*), but was sensitive to changes in touch. It was called *"a consolation in grief and a friend in joy."* [20]

[15] *New Grove Dictionary of Music and Musicians*, s.v. "Clavichord" (London: Macmillan, 1980), vol. 4, 466.

[16] Ibid., s.v. "Empfindsamkeit," vol. 6, 157.

[17] Ibid., quoting C.P.E. Bach, 158.

[18] Ottenberg, *C.P.E. Bach*, 3.

[19] Arthur Loesser, *Men, Women & Pianos* (New York: Simon and Schuster, 1954), 61.

[20] Dr. Mark Zilberquit, *The Book of the Piano*, trans. by Yuri S. Shirokov (Neptune, NJ: Paganiniana Publications, Inc., 1987), 15.

*"Keyboardists whose chief asset is mere technique…overwhelm our hearing without satisfying it and stun the mind without moving it…"*

C.P.E. Bach[21]

# Fantasia in G Major

Carl Philipp Emanuel Bach
(1714–1788)

[21] Kimball, *The Music Lover's Quotation Book*, 61.

**Wilhelm Friedemann Bach** (1710–1784) was the oldest, and perhaps the most gifted, son of J. S. Bach. At a young age he assisted his father with rehearsals, taught and copied music. He completed his education in math, philosophy and law at the University in Leipzig.

- Known as an organ virtuoso, he became the Court organist in Dresden. Later employed by the city of Halle, he abruptly left without notice. His final years were spent erratically teaching, composing and giving concerts. He died in poverty.

# "Learned" and New Style Elements Combined

Many composers during the late 18th century shifted between **"learned" (old) and new style elements**, sometimes within the same work. W. F. Bach was extremely successful in this.

- The following *Aria* opens with a balanced phrase structure divided into **short segments**. **Melody** is prominent **in a light texture** typical of the newer *style galant*.

- The second (**B**) section is in a more **"learned" or contrapuntal style** used by his father and other Baroque composers. Measure 19 begins a passage with a **motive and two sequences** where both hands are equal in importance.

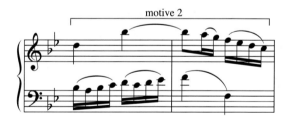

- The *Polonaise in D Minor* (page 34) is an example of the *empfindsamkeit,* or **sensitive style** so associated with his brother, C.P.E. Bach.

This aria combines new *style galant* elements with more "learned" or contrapuntal style.
See page 31 for musical examples from this piece.

Wilhelm Friedemann Bach
(1710–1784)

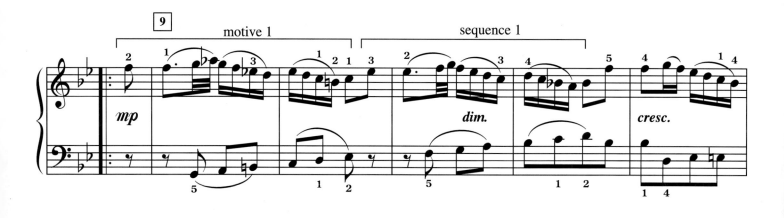

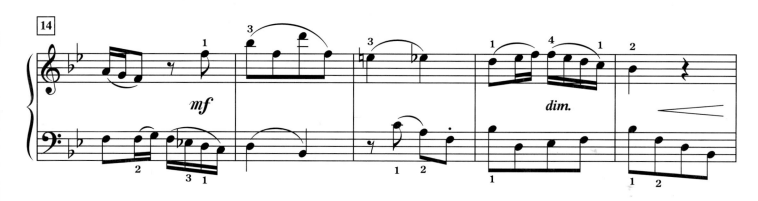

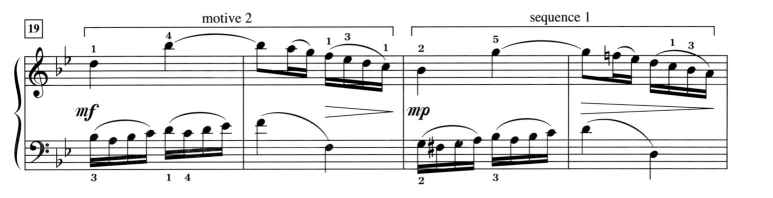

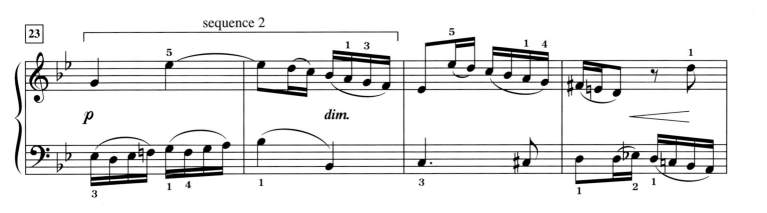

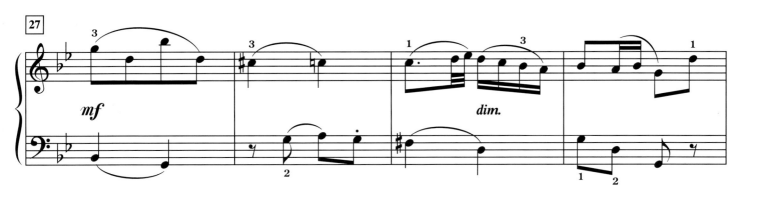

This is from a set of 12 polonaises by **W. F. Bach.** Sighing chromaticism, daring harmonies, and abrupt dynamic shifts show the **sensitive style** in this regal dance form. An early edition, based on performances by **Johann Forkel** (1749–1818), stated that polonaises in minor keys should be played *adagio* with slow, melodic appoggiaturas.

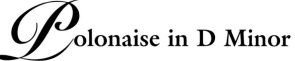

# Polonaise in D Minor

Wilhelm Friedemann Bach
(1710–1784)

# London, a Musical Hub

In the late 18th century, London was the leading city in **public musical life.** Music at the Court was less important, and few aristocratic families in England had household musicians. Music was needed for outdoor parties, indoor gatherings, amateur music societies, operas, and public concert halls. Native and continental musicians filled the demand.

## Music Publishing in London

- Having **musical skills** was seen as a necessary **social accomplishment**, creating **upper- and middle-class amateurs**[23] who needed "easy" printed music to sing and play, affordable instruments and music lessons.

- Modern music publishing was established in London around 1700 and soon became a significant industry. Professional critics wrote concert reviews in journals, instruction books were published with helpful advice for amateurs, and music catalogs advertised Sonatas, Lessons, Methods and Collections (for harpsichord or piano) by leading composers of the day.

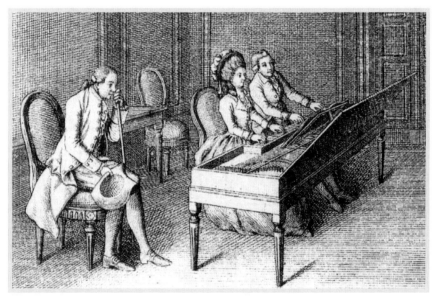

*Title page for* Six Sonatas for Two Persons at One Clavier.

*A duet being played on a square piano.*

*1781 engraving by Johann August Rosmaesler for Franz Seydelmann*

## Keyboard Sonata and Sonatina

The term **sonata** had different meanings at different time periods but always referred to an instrumental piece that became associated with the keyboard. When first used in 1669, **sonatina**, a small sonata, was linked with amateurs and teaching.

- **Some 18th-century sonatas** were played by keyboard virtuosos in concerts, but most were intended for domestic use, sometimes with an accompanying instrumentalist.

- By 1750, **sonata** referred most often to a **three-movement** plan of **fast–slow–fast**. In England, sonatas were sometimes called **lessons**, implying self-improvement.

---

[22] Derek Watson, ed. introduction and selection, *Dictionary of Musical Quotations* (Ware Hertfordshire: Cumberland House, Wordsworth Editions Ltd., 1994), 79.

[23] Derived from the Latin word "to love," a musical amateur (lover of music), refers to one pursuing it as a pastime rather than a profession.

**William Duncombe** was an English harpsichordist, pianist and organist. This sonatina is from his *First Book of Progressive Lessons for the Harpsichord and Piano-forte* published in London around 1780.

# Sonatina in C Major

William Duncombe
18th century

Intrada

In most published versions of the *Fanfare Minuet,* measures 17–19 are exactly the same as measures 1–3. The added notes in measures 17–19 are in Duncombe's original edition and help to build excitement in the final fanfare.

Fanfare Minuet

# The Hunt
## Gigue

(a) The editor suggests that the appoggiaturas be played before the beat.

*"His [Johann Christian Bach] keyboard works were such 'as ladies can execute with little trouble.'"*
Dr. Charles Burney (1726–1814), 18th-century music historian[24]

## Piano Manufacturing in London

- In 1760, a group of German instrument makers immigrated to London, including **Johann Zumpe** (1726–1790). He built a successful business manufacturing square pianos for the home, and *"he could not make them fast enough to gratify the craving of the public,"* according to Dr. Burney.[25]

- In 1768, Johann Christian Bach performed a **public solo piano concert** on a **five-octave Zumpe** giving it public credibility and exposure.

- By 1780, there were two types of grand pianos dominating Europe: the English (Broadwood) and the German or Viennese (Stein). Each model had a unique mechanical action.

**Johann Christian Bach** (1735–1782), the youngest son of Johann Sebastian and Anna Magdalena Bach, was first taught music by his father and then by his older brother, Carl Philipp Emanuel, in Berlin. Known as a keyboard virtuoso, J.C. went to Italy to study opera, composed church music there, and became the Milan Cathedral organist.

- Success with his operas in Turin and Naples led him to London in 1762 to conduct Italian opera. Appointed Music Master to the Queen in London, he performed, taught, published Lessons and Sonatas, and organized public concerts.

- Making London his home, he had great influence on many contemporary musicians, including the eight-year-old Mozart who spent a year there.

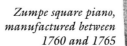

*Zumpe square piano, manufactured between 1760 and 1765*

A Sunday Concert at the Home of Charles Burney *(a satirical engraving). Dr. Burney, at front right, could not stop gossiping, even during the concert.*

*Dr. Burney traveled Europe and in 1771 published* The Present State of Music in France and Italy, a General History. *Other regions were covered in 1773 and 1775 volumes.*

[24] James Galway, *Music in Time* (New York: Harry N. Abrams, Inc., 1983), 131.
[25] David Crombie, *Piano, A Photographic History* (San Francisco: GPI Books, 1995), 18.

This toccata is from *Introduction to the Piano, a Method for the Forte-Piano*, co-authored by **J. C. Bach** and **Francesco Pasquale Ricci** (1732–1817). First published in Paris in 1786, *Introduction* contains 100 pieces that emphasize technical skills. **One motive and its sequential patterns** dominate this toccata. The motive enters a second time in measure 11, this time in the left hand together with a new right-hand voice. This complete pattern is then sequenced several times.

# Toccata

Johann Christian Bach
(1735–1782)

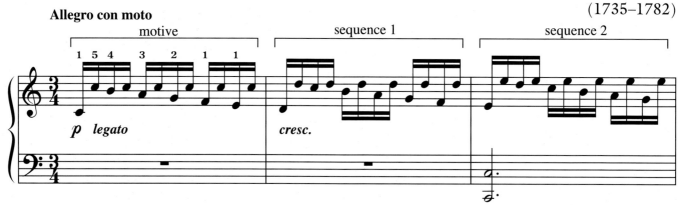

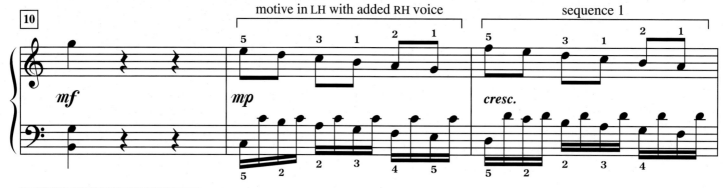

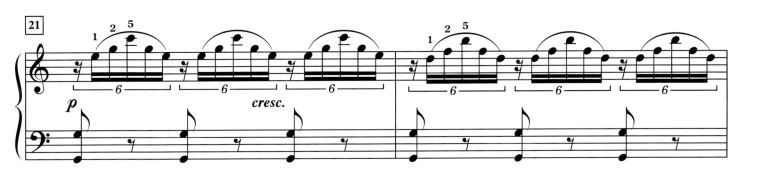

Taught mainly by his father, Johann Sebastian, **Johann Christoph Friedrich Bach** (1732–1795) took his first position as a court musician in Bückenburg around the time of his father's death. After becoming *Konzertmeister* there, he composed, produced and conducted many oratorios, cantatas, symphonies, operas and chamber music.

- Taking a leave from the Court in 1778, he and his son, **Wilhelm Friedrich Ernst** (1759–1845), traveled to London to visit J.C.F's brother Johann Christian. While there, J.C.F. purchased a pianoforte and a great deal of music. They also attended many musical events, including J.C. Bach's new opera. J.C.F. returned home, leaving his son in London to continue his musical training.

- An outstanding virtuoso, most of J.C.F. Bach's published keyboard pieces were short and in *style galant* with a few in the "expressive" style.

## Anglaise

The **anglaise** (English dance) was a term used on the Continent to describe all dance music thought to have originated in England. Late in Louis XIV's (1638–1715) reign, French dancing masters imported English **country dances** to enliven court balls.

Originating in English villages, it was a simpler, more "natural," yet energetic dance. Second in popularity only to the minuet during the 18th century, it was slightly modified in Louis XIV's Court. There it was known as **contredanse** (counter/opposite) since couples faced each other, rather than the King, as they danced in lines.

*Country Dance by William Hogarth (1697–1764).*
*Hogarth was a popular painter and engraver who satirized many aspects of English society in his art.*

# Anglaise

Johann Christoph Friedrich Bach
(1732–1795)

# Musical Austria

The German **Habsburgs** were the most powerful royal family of Europe, controlling vast territories of land acquired through battles and shrewd marriages. During the 13th century, they gained control of Austria and ruled until the end of World War I (1918).

- **Leopold I** (1640–1705) married a Spanish princess. His daughter, **Maria Theresa** (1717–1780) married the French Duke of Lorraine (1708–1765) and they had 16 children. A son, **Joseph II** (1741–1790), married an Italian princess, and daughter **Marie-Antoinette** (1755–1793) married Louis XVI (1754–1793) of France.

- Also **patrons of the arts,** the Habsburgs imported Italian operas as well as other foreign artists, composers and performers. Many were **accomplished musicians** themselves with Leopold I a highly skilled composer, conductor and performer.

Photo: Kunsthistorisches Museum

*Emperor Joseph II of Austria with two of his sisters. He was a good singer, viola, cello and keyboard player, and often accompanied performances at Court.*

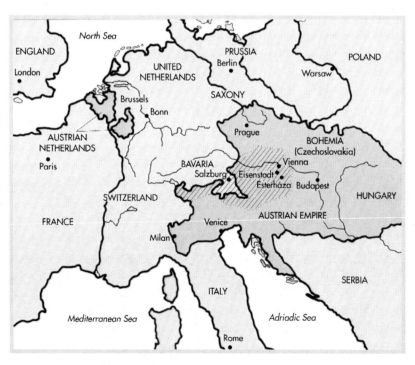

The Austrian Empire around 1780

Austria Today

- The size of the **Austrian Empire** helped it develop a unique musical style during the Classical period. It became the **melting pot** for the Germanic culture of central Europe, the music and vocal style of Northern Italy, the cultural and folk elements of Hungary and the Slavs, and the brilliant wind playing of Bohemia (today's Czech Republic) with touches of French and Spanish ingredients.

[26]Richard Rickett, *A Brief Survey of Austrian History* (Vienna: Georg Prachner Verlag, 1966), 27.

**Carl Ditters von Dittersdorf's** father was a costumer at the Imperial Court in Vienna. Having grown up in that environment, Carl was privileged with an excellent education. He composed all forms of music and his over 100 symphonies have been compared to Haydn's. He wrote **20 English dances** for keyboard.

# *E*nglish Dance

Carl Ditters von Dittersdorf
(1739–1799)

(a) The editor suggests that the appoggiatura be played before the beat.

**Johann Baptist Vanhal**, although born in Bohemia, studied music in Vienna with Carl Ditters von Dittersdorf and established himself there as a teacher and composer. He is known to have played in a string quartet with Dittersdorf, Haydn and Mozart.

# Allegretto in A Major

Johann Baptist Vanhal (1739–1813)
Op. 41, No. 12

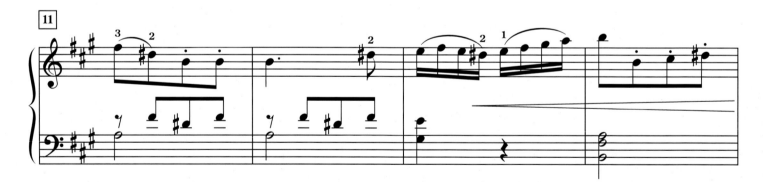

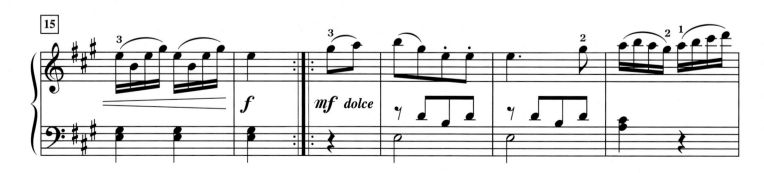

# ienna, Musical Capital of Europe

Capital of the Austrian Empire, **Vienna** was also the **musical capital of Europe** during the Classical period. Around 1750 it had a French emperor (husband of **Maria Theresa**), an Italian Court poet and composer, performances of French-style operas and ballets, and concerts by Belgian, German and Austrian instrumentalists, making it a **cosmopolitan city**.

Maria Theresa began her reign in 1740. A trained singer with a great love for the theater, she soon divided her group of about 130 musicians into two smaller groups; one performed sacred music and the other operas. The Court eventually took over the management of Vienna's two leading theaters.

When theaters closed during Lent, public concerts were allowed. **Public subscriptions** were frequently sold in advance to cover expenses for the musician who organized the event. People of all social classes attended the theater, operas, ballets and public concerts.

Nobility from the entire Empire had palaces in Vienna as well as other residences and estates in the various regions. One estimate was that 8,000 aristocrats were residing in Vienna in the 1780s since all spent part of each year there. Great rivalry developed among the aristocrats for the finest orchestras and musicians.

*Engraving by Karl Schütz (1785) of St. Michael's Square in Vienna showing the Burgtheater, where many of Mozart's operas, symphonies and piano concertos were premiered.*

[27] Neil Butterworth, *Haydn, Illustrated Lives of the Great Composers* (New York: Omnibus Press, 1987), 73.

## Patronage and the "Viennese Masters"

Music was very important for status to all social classes. Wealthy aristocrats hired musicians as **part of their household** and it was common to see advertisements in Viennese newspapers for servants who could also play a musical instrument. Although there was some economic security, a professional musician's rank was little better than that of a servant.

Some patrons (frequently middle-class) would **commission a favorite composer** to write a work for a specific event, or hire musicians for a **single performance**. Other aristocrats organized concerts and paid leading musicians to participate.

- **Franz Joseph Haydn** spent over 30 years as Director of Court Music for the Esterházy family  He had a restrictive contract, wore a servant's uniform, and said that he sat at their dinner table "below the salt." Since ambassadors, royalty, and even the Empress Maria Theresa visited the Esterházy estates, Haydn eventually became very famous and financially independent.

- **Wolfgang Amadeus Mozart** left his position at the Court in Salzburg and never secured another Court position. As a freelance musician, his income came from performing, publishing, fulfilling commissions, and giving lessons. Although he had some success with his operas and his subscription concert series (where he performed his piano concertos), he died in poverty.

- **Ludwig van Beethoven** had a contract with three Viennese noblemen who agreed to pay him a salary to remain in Vienna and compose. He was not seen as a servant, but was recognized and rewarded because of his extraordinary musical gifts. By the early 1800s, he was offered more commissions than he could accept. He boasted that he could set a high price and get it.

*The Palace at Eszterháza, Hungary, where Haydn was employed.*

*"There was no one near me to upset or torment me, so I was forced to become original."*

Haydn on his years at the Eszterháza Palace[28]

## Franz Joseph Haydn

Haydn was highly respected and his music was known throughout Europe during his lifetime. He stated that what he had accomplished was a result of great need.

- At age six, he was sent from his small Austrian town to live with his cousin who was a musician and teacher. After two years of intense study, he was accepted as a choirboy at St. Stephen's Cathedral in Vienna.

- There he was educated and instructed in singing, violin and keyboard. During his nine years in the choir, Haydn said he had two lessons in theory and none in composition. He taught himself by carefully studying the music he heard and sang.

- Dismissed when his voice changed, he was without money, a job or a place to live. He taught and accompanied, played the violin, composed for chamber music evenings in aristocratic homes, and for a time was a servant to an opera composer.

- He gradually became known in musical circles, and in 1761 was hired to conduct the orchestra of the Hungarian Prince Paul Esterházy (1711–1762).

- At this time the Esterházy family owned about 25 palaces and castles and one and a half million acres of land. A choir, orchestra, military band and actors were part of the household staff. Haydn was in charge of all musical instruments and musicians and was to compose and rehearse music desired for any occasion.

- Prince Nicholas Esterházy (1714–1790) spent the equivalent of four million dollars building the Esterháza Palace that he patterned after Versailles. Designed for entertaining, the opera house seated 400, there were two concert halls, a marionette theater and 126 guest rooms. The family employed Haydn until his death.

*Engraving of Franz Joseph Haydn (1792)*
*by Luigi Schiavotti*

---

[28] Alan Kendall, *The Chronicle of Classical Music* (London: Thames and Hudson Ltd., 1994), 99.

This *Presto in G Major* shows the optimistic spirit common in **Haydn's** music. The opening section is based upon a rhythmic motive that is expanded and then repeated. The G minor section (measures 25–48) has a contrasting texture.

This same music is found **twice in his 62 keyboard sonatas**. It is the **last** of a three-movement sonata (H. XVI/G1; L. 4), and the **first** of another three-movement sonata (H. XVI/11; L. 5).

# Presto in G Major

Franz Joseph Haydn
(1732–1809)

# Minuet in C Minor

Franz Joseph Haydn
(1732–1809)

(a) The editor suggests that the appoggiaturas be played before the beat.

*"I tell you before God, as an honest man,
that your son is the greatest composer I know,
either personally or by repute."*

Franz Joseph Haydn in a letter to Leopold Mozart[29]

### Wolfgang Amadeus Mozart

- Mozart was a genius from birth, playing keyboard melodies at age 3, performing publicly and composing by age 5. At age 6, he was taken on his first concert tour where he performed with his older sister, **Nannerl** (1751–1829).

- A report of a performance at age 7 tells he *"could play in an adult manner, improvise in various styles, accompany at sight, play with a cloth covering the keyboard, add a bass to a given theme, and name any note that was sounded."*[30]

- By age 8 he had performed at the Courts in Bavaria and Salzburg, for Maria Theresa in Vienna, Louis XV (1710–1744) at Versailles, and for George III (1738–1820) in London. In 1770, he was honored by Pope Clement XIV (1705–1774) in Rome. He was able to assimilate everything from his extensive travels to France, Italy and England into his compositions.

- At a program in Italy (prepared by professional musicians) he performed as soloist in a piano concerto followed by a solo sonata, both of which he read at sight. He then added variations and transposed the sonata. Next he was given words for an aria that he instantly composed and sang while accompanying himself. He was given a theme and improvised both a sonata and fugue on it. He also played violin in a trio and conducted one of his symphonies. Mozart was 14.

- He and Franz Joseph Haydn became friends, and although Mozart was much younger, the two exchanged ideas and influenced each other in their musical compositions.

*A 1763 engraving of Mozart at the keyboard
with his father, Leopold (1719–1787), playing
the violin and his sister, Nannerl, singing.*

[29]Crofton & Fraser, *Musical Quotations*, 97.

[30]*New Grove Dictionary, s.v.* "Mozart, Wolfgang Amadeus," vol. 12, 681.

Composed while on tour in Zurich when Mozart was 10 years old, he never gave this
piece a title. On that trip, he also performed in Amsterdam, Brussels, Paris and Munich.

# Klavierstücke in F Major

Wolfgang Amadeus Mozart
(1756–1791)
K. 33B

**Mozart** originally wrote this piece for wind instruments. Published before 1800, it is believed to be his own keyboard arrangement. The lyric expressiveness of the opening theme shows Mozart's great **melodic gifts**.

# Andante in C Major

Wolfgang Amadeus Mozart
(1756–1791

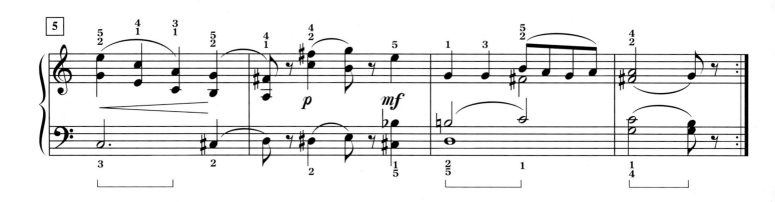

[31] Charles Rosen, *The Sonata Forms* (New York: W. W. Norton & Co., 1988), 177.

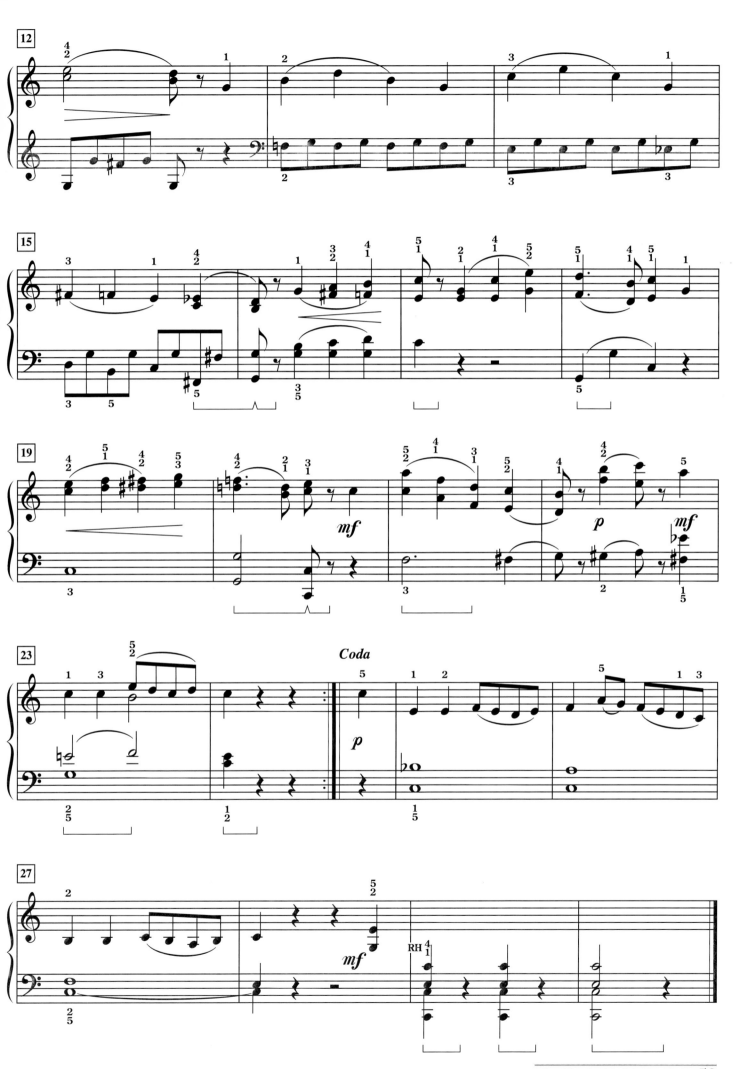

This was written as a joke for Barbara von Ployer, one of Mozart's students. It is believed to be a parody of the opening of his *Concerto in G Major*, K. 453, which he composed for her.

# Marche funèbre del Signor Maestro Contrapunto
## (Funeral March for Masterful Mr. Counterpoint)

Wolfgang Amadeus Mozart
(1756–1791)
K. 453a

*"Prince, what you are, you are by the accident of birth; what I am, I am of myself. There...will be thousands of princes. There is only one Beethoven."*

Letter to Prince Lichnowsky, 1806[32]

## Ludwig van Beethoven

With the piano greatly improved, a public that wanted to hear and play music, and a wide variety of established instrumental forms (that unlimited by words were capable of expressing an infinite range of emotions), the stage was set for **Beethoven**.

- Ludwig was the third generation of court musicians in **Bonn**. His father, a singer, saw that he had good musical training, and by age 11, he was an assistant to the Court organist. By 13, he had published works.

- Beethoven made a brief visit to Vienna where it is believed **he met Mozart** and had a few lessons with him. In 1792, Beethoven returned to Vienna to study with Haydn and spent the rest of his life there. When he left Bonn, Count Waldstein said, *"You shall receive Mozart's spirit from Haydn's hands."* [33]

- From Vienna, Beethoven toured and performed as a piano virtuoso in palaces of the aristocracy, private homes, and in public concerts. He published works by subscription and was at the height of success when he began to go deaf. His increasing deafness forced him to stop performing and to compose full-time.

- He was kindhearted, but frank to the point of rudeness. He had an uncontrollable temper, and such sloppy personal habits that he lived 80 different places in Vienna. His genius ultimately overcame his eccentric and erratic behavior.

Photo: AKG London

*When they met in Vienna, Mozart reportedly said, "Keep an eye on that young man [Beethoven]. Someday he will make a big splash in the world."* [34]

---

[32] Crofton & Fraser, *Musical Quotations*, 15.

[33] *New Grove Dictionary*, s.v. "Beethoven, Ludwig van," vol. 2, 357.

[34] Kimball, *The Music Lover's Quotation Book*, 40.

*"When writing for the public, one undoubtedly writes most beautifully—and also rapidly."*
Ludwig van Beethoven[35]

**Ludwig van Beethoven** composed this waltz in 1824 for publication in an album of dance pieces. It shows his interest in the unique sound and color possibilities of the piano and his use of unusual pedal effects.

# Waltz in E-flat Major

Ludwig van Beethoven
(1770–1827)
WoO 84

[35] Crofton & Fraser, *Musical Quotations*, 15.

ⓐ Beethoven indicated to depress the pedal here but did not say where to lift it. The editor suggests holding the damper pedal down, without change, throughout the section to give the effect of a bagpipe.

ⓑ The editor suggests that the appoggiaturas be played before the beat.

This folkdance is the **theme** from a set of four variations for **piano with an added flute or violin**. The **accompanied sonata,** extremely popular during the 18th century, was *"essentially an amateur domestic medium, designed for lady pianists of moderate skill and gentlemen string-players of yet more slender accomplishment."*[36]

# Ländler
(Tyrolean Air)

Ludwig van Beethoven
(1770–1827)
Op. 107, No. 1

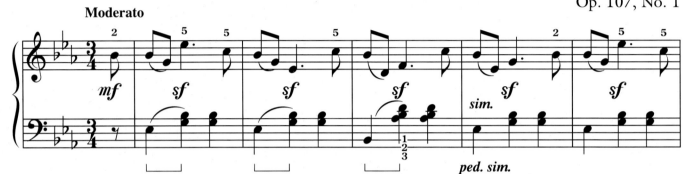

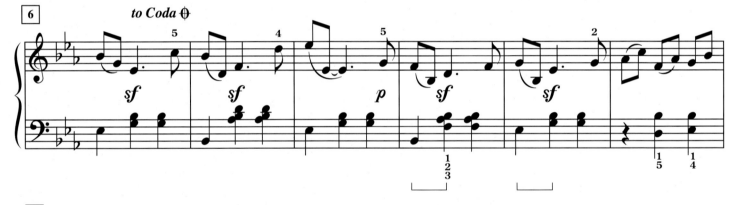

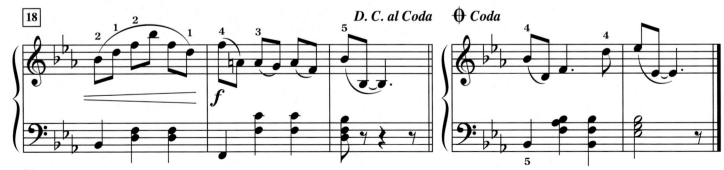

[36] James Parakilas and others, *Piano Roles*, quoting from "Concert Life in London"
(New Haven: Yale University Press, 1999), 26.